Ready, Freddy! READER

P9-CSG-377

LEVEL 2

DEVELOPING READER • 250-750 WORDS

Easter Egg Hunt

by ABBY KLEIN

illustrated by JOHN McKINLEY

SCHOLASTIC INC.

New York   Toronto   London   Auckland   Sydney
Mexico City   New Delhi   Hong Kong   Buenos Aires

To Amy—
The one who always had the biggest
and most beautiful Easter basket.
Love—A.K.

To A.J., with love—J.M.

ISBN-13: 978-0-545-09931-8
ISBN-10: 0-545-09931-5

Text copyright © 2009 by Abby Klein
Illustrations copyright © 2009 by John McKinley

12 11 10 9 8 7 6 5 4 3 2 1   9 10 11 12 13 14/0

Printed in the U.S.A.
First printing, March 2009

It was one week until Easter.

I was shopping with my mom,
and I saw a sign.

"The Easter Egg Hunt prize is a huge
chocolate bunny," I said. "This year I am going
to win it."

"Maybe you will," said my mom.

"Oh, I hope I do," I said.

The week went by really slowly.
It seemed like Saturday would never come.
I waited
      and waited
            and waited.

Finally it came.

On Saturday morning, I jumped out of bed.

I pulled my Easter basket out of my closet.

I made an extra big one this year.

It has to hold a lot of eggs because I am going to win that grand prize.

I called for my sister, Suzie. "Suzie!"

"What?" Suzie shouted.

"Can you come here for a second?"

Suzie walked slowly into my room.

"What do you want, Sharkbreath?" she said.
"I was sleeping, and you woke me up."

"I need your help to win," I said.

"What makes you think you're
going to win?"

"I really want to," I said.

"But what about Max?" Suzie asked.

"You mean the biggest bully
in the whole first grade?" I asked.

"Yes, him. He beats you in everything."

"He wins because he cheats," I said. "But this year I'm going to beat him. Now that you're too old to go on the hunt, can you help me?"

"Only if you share some of the chocolate bunny with me," Suzie said.

"But . . ."

"Deal?" Suzie asked, holding up her pinky for a pinky swear.

"Fine. Deal," I said, and we locked pinkies.

"Last year you found the most eggs.
Tell me where they hide them," I said.

"Usually they hide a bunch of eggs
in the sandbox and at the top of the slide,"
my sister said.

"Thanks, Suzie. You're the best sister
in the whole world!"

"I know," Suzie said, smiling.
"Good luck, Freddy. Go beat Max."

A little later, we went to the park.
All the kids were there with their baskets.
Chloe's basket had pink ribbons
and bows all over it.

Jessie had baseballs and baseball cards on her basket.

Robbie had a basket with little plastic animals on it.

"Cool basket," I said to Robbie.

"Thanks," he said. "I like your basket, too."

My basket was decorated with shark teeth because I love sharks.

"Okay, everybody," a lady called.
"It's time to start the hunt."

I looked around, but I didn't see Max.
Maybe it was my lucky day.
Maybe Max was not coming.

But Max ran up.

"Wait for me!" he yelled.

He was carrying the biggest basket
I had ever seen.

"You're just in time," said the lady.

"Great," said Max.

Then he turned to me and whispered, "I'm going to beat you again, Freddy. Just watch."

20

"Don't listen to him," said Jessie and Robbie. "We know you can beat him."

Then the lady said, "Whoever finds the most eggs will win this huge chocolate bunny."

"Is everybody ready?" the lady yelled.

"Yes!" we all shouted.

"On your mark, get set, go!"

We all ran.

I found three eggs right away.

One was under the bench.

Two were hidden in a bush.

But when I was in the sandbox,

Max took one from my basket.

"Hey, you can't do that!" I yelled.

"Oh, yeah? Watch me," he said.

He ran off.

"Cheater!" I yelled after him.

"Don't worry," said Jessie.

"Cheaters never win."

I had to find more eggs.
I didn't want Max to win.

I went back to the sandbox
and I found six more eggs.

I found two by the water fountain,

four at the top of the slide,

and one by the old tree.

"Time's up!" the lady yelled.
"Bring your baskets to me."
She counted Max's eggs first.
"Fourteen eggs. Wow! That's a lot."
"I'm going to win," said Max, smiling.

The lady counted the eggs in the other baskets.

No one had as many as Max.

My basket was the last one.

"Good luck," whispered Jessie.

"Eleven,
      twelve,
            thirteen,
                  fourteen . . ."
I held my breath.
She reached in the basket
and pulled out one more.
"Fifteen!"
I jumped up and down.
"I won, I won!"
"It's not fair," Max mumbled.
"It's very fair," said Jessie.
"Cheaters never win."

"Congratulations, Freddy," said the lady. "You win the grand prize."

She handed me the huge chocolate bunny. I licked my lips.

"Thanks," I said. "This is the best Easter ever!"